Disney's
My Very First Winnie the Pooh ™

Gopher's Day Out

Adaptation Cassandra Case   Illustrated by John Kurtz

SCHOLASTIC INC.

New York Toronto London Auckland Sydney
Mexico City New Delhi Hong Kong Buenos Aires

ISBN 0-7172-8895-1

Copyright © 1999 by Disney Enterprises, Inc. All rights reserved.
Published by Scholastic Inc., 555 Broadway, New York, NY 10012,
by arrangement with Disney Licensed Publishing.
SCHOLASTIC and associated logos are trademarks
and/or registered trademarks of Scholastic Inc.

Based on the Pooh stories by A. A. Milne
(copyright The Pooh Properties Trust).

12 11 10 9 8 7 6 5 4 3 2 1   1 2 3 4 5 6/0

Printed in the U.S.A.   56

First Scholastic printing, November 2001

"Helloo-oo, Gopher?" Pooh called into one of Gopher's holes. "We're having a picnic and I'm inviting you!"

"Sssayy, Pooh!" Gopher popped up, whistling through his teeth as he spoke. "That sssoundsss like fun, but I can't posssibly. I have jussst *one* more passsageway to dig to connect *all* my tunnelsss!"

"Oh, I see," said Pooh, even though he really didn't see.

"Maybe nexssst time!" whistled Gopher and he popped back down his hole.

"Hmmm," Pooh wondered. "Why would anyone want to dig a tunnel instead of come to a *picnic*?"

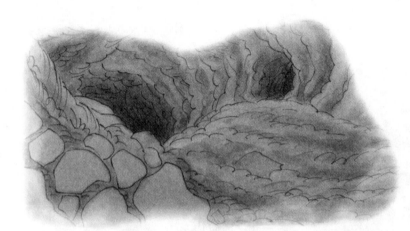

"Well, thisss isss my big day!" Gopher whistled to himself. "When thisss tunnel isss finished, I can run from one tunnel to the next under the *whole* Hundred-Acre Wood!"

Gopher scratched a large X on the wall of earth in front of him.

"X marksss the ssspot to begin!" he said. He took his pick-axe and swung it into the middle of the X on the count of "1-2-3."

But when Gopher pulled his pick-axe back out – *SsssppllOOOOSH!!* – a whole lot of water followed.

"Oooppsss! The river'sss come in to visssit!" yelped Gopher, as the river water carried him down the nearest tunnel.

"I guesss I wasss a tiny bit too clossse to the river," whistled Gopher as he rode along. "I mussst've made a missstake in my calculationsss."

Meanwhile, up in the sunny Hundred-Acre Wood, Pooh and his friends spread a blanket on the soft green grass and set out yummy things to eat.

"What I like best about picnics," said Pooh happily, "is the PICNIC!"

"Same with me!" agreed Tigger. "And I like the food, too! Hoo hoo *hoo*!"

"Too bad Gopher couldn't join us,"
said Piglet.

"Yes," agreed Pooh. "But he's busy. He's
connecting all his tunnels."

"Not even *I* can be busy *all* the time!" said
Rabbit. "Once in a while Gopher should forget
his excavations and take a vacation."

"Oh, I believe Gopher likes
digging so much that he doesn't
want an exca-vacation,"
said Pooh, who had settled
down with a honey jar.

Owl started to explain that "digging" and "excavation" are two different words that mean the same thing, when all of a sudden there was a gurgly noise underneath the picnic.

"Oh, excuse me!" chuckled Pooh, thinking it was his tummy enjoying the picnic.

But the gurgling *wasn't* from Pooh's tummy – it was from the water in Gopher's tunnels!

Inside a tunnel, right under the picnic, Gopher and the water whooshed along. Then the water found one of Gopher's holes and was in such a hurry to get out, that it shoved Gopher up ahead of it with a *POP!*

Up Gopher sailed into the air! Then down he plopped into the middle of the picnic!

"Hoo hoo *hoo*!" cried Tigger. "That was some BOUNCE, buddy-boy!"

"Sssorry," said Gopher, taking a bowl off his head. "I made a sssmall missstake . . . ."

"Oh, that's all right," said Pooh. "It's never a mistake to drop in on friends!"

"Are your tunnels all connected now?" asked Piglet.

"Sssort of," answered Gopher.

"Can I go in them, Mama?" cried Roo, hopping up and down.
"No, Roo, dear," said Kanga. "Only tunneling animals can go."

"They're full of mud, Roo," Gopher said. "Even *I'm* not going back. It's a sssticky messs."

"But tunnels is where gophers belong!" said Tigger.
"Where will you go?" said Eeyore.
"I think I'll ssstay above ground and visssit my friendsss!" replied Gopher.

First Gopher visited Pooh. Next day, when Pooh wanted honey from a bee tree, Gopher said he would help. So he dug a hole under the tall, hollow tree.

"But Gopher," said Pooh, "the honey is at the *top* of the tree."

"Climb *inssside* the tree-hollow from the hole," said Gopher, "then crawl up to the honey."

"Oh! I see!" said Pooh. Everyone watched Pooh disappear inside the tree. They could hear Pooh's humming going up and up. Then they heard a buzzing sound, coming down. Pooh scrambled back out.

"*Bees!*" he cried, and everyone ran away.

A little later, Gopher wandered into Rabbit's garden. Rabbit was hoeing his rows of carrots.

"What'sss that you're doing?" asked Gopher.

"I'm digging weeds," Rabbit answered. "It gives the carrots more room to breathe and grow."

"Sssay now," said Gopher, "I can help with that!" Before Rabbit could answer, Gopher dug down under the garden bed. "They can breathe underneath, now, too!" he called up to Rabbit. "Want me to pick you sssome?"

"Gopher, wait!" cried Rabbit. "Carrots need *earth* under them to *grow* in!"

"Ooopsss, sssorry!" said Gopher.

That afternoon, it looked like rain. Gopher found Eeyore looking sadly at his roof.

"Ah, me. I'll get all wet again," sighed Eeyore.

"I don't do roofsss," said Gopher. "But, sssay! How 'bout a basssement to go in and be out of the rain?"

In a flash, Gopher dug an enormous cellar. The little house of twigs and sticks gave a small creak. Then it fell – CRASH! – into the bottom of the cellar.

"Well . . ." said Eeyore, "I suppose it'll be a good place to store twigs and sticks."

"I'm sssorry, Eeyore," mumbled Gopher. "Thisss isss not a good day!"

"*I* think," said Pooh, with a glance out the window, "that our river is getting too full of itself."

"Oh, my goodness!" screeched Rabbit. "It's going to flood our houses!" He yanked open the door to get a better look and there stood Gopher, dripping wet.

"I wanted to apologize . . ." Gopher began.

"No time, Gopher," squeaked Piglet. "The river's going to wash us all away!"

Gopher looked at the river. Suddenly, he knew exactly what to do. He raced off and dropped out of sight down a nearby tunnel.

efore Eeyore could
think what to say,
Gopher had scuttled off.
The first big drops of
rain fell. Eeyore decided to go see if
he could find shelter at Piglet's. He just barely
arrived as it began thundering and pouring rain.
Pooh, Tigger, and Rabbit were already there.
Eeyore told them about the cellar.

"Gopher is making problems," said Rabbit.

"It's 'cause he can't stop himself from
diggin'," Tigger pointed out. "But he
should be diggin' in his own tunnels.
That's what *I* think!"

"What do you think, Pooh?"
asked Piglet.

"I think," said Pooh, with a glance out the window, "that our river is getting too full of itself."

"Oh, my goodness!" screeched Rabbit. "It's going to flood our houses!" He yanked open the door to get a better look and there stood Gopher, dripping wet.

"I wanted to apologize . . ." Gopher began.

"No time, Gopher," squeaked Piglet. "The river's going to wash us all away!"

Gopher looked at the river. Suddenly, he knew exactly what to do. He raced off and dropped out of sight down a nearby tunnel.

Next day, Gopher went to work clearing out his tunnels. Pooh helped him by carrying mud away in an extra helmet and dumping it back into the river. When they took a break, they headed to Pooh's house for a smackerel of honey.

"Oh, Pooh!" said Gopher. "I sssure did misss my tunnelsss. It's ssso good to be back where I belong!"